Santa's Famous

Incredible

Flying Reindeer

By Joe Moore

As Told To By Santa Claus

Other Books by Joe Moore:

The Santa Claus Trilogy

Believe Again, The North Pole Chronicles
Faith, Hope & Reindeer
Glaciers Melt & Mountains Smoke

Santa's Elf Series

Santa's World
Jamie Hardrock, Chief Mining Elf
Shelley Wrapitup, Master Design Elf
Keeney Eagleye, Naughty/Nice List Manager
Sarah Buttons, Master Doll Maker
Ford MacHarley, Master Wheelsmith

Return of the Birds

The Faces of Krampus

The Santa Claus Enigma

The North Pole Press
Smoky Mountains, Tennessee

Santa's Famous, Incredible, Flying Reindeer
by Joe Moore
Copyright 2011

ISBN #978-0-9787129-1-4

Information about and for this book may be obtained by
contacting The North Pole Press at:
info@thenorthpolepress.com

Message from Santa Claus

I t has been another exciting year, as most of them are. Everyone did very well during the last Christmas Eve run, and of course my horse did his part for the Feast of St. Nicholas.

What's that? Didn't you know Santa had a horse? My father had used our horse, Amerigo, long before we discovered reindeer. My Dad used to ride Amerigo up from Spain into France, England and the Netherlands delivering candies and toys in shoes that were left outside to dry. He would do this on the Eve of St. Nicholas Feast Day in honor of our ancestor St. Nicholas.

Every December 6th, towns throughout Europe have big festivals and celebrations, and my ancestors and I would give presents to children to let them know we were still around. It is not as big as our Christmas Eve run, but it is still a significant celebration, that we love to do.

But I digress, this book is about the most famous of our reindeer. Rarely do people see our reindeer on Christmas Eve, and I believed it was about time that I expounded on them. Here you will meet each reindeer, see their picture, learn how they got their names and even how often I use them.

Now to make something clear, these are NOT the only reindeer I use on my runs. Far from it, but these are the names that nearly everyone knows (except Torch, who I will explain later). I have many more reindeer and depending on the interest of this book, I may come out with another concerning my lesser known, but equally necessary, other flying reindeer. Refer to these reindeer as my second string, if you like.

Before I introduce you to them personally, let me answer one of the most common questions I receive every year. How do my reindeer fly? No, it's not fairy dust or magic words, and it's not magic corn, oats, hay or carrots. It's alfalfa, but it is an extraordinary kind of alfalfa.

It happened a long time past when the elves lived all around the globe. These events took place before they all gathered for the Great Migration and settlement to the North Pole (see *Believe Again, The North Pole Chronicles*). In an exceptional site which is now a closely guarded secret, some elves sowed a blend of alfalfa seed that grew with an extraordinary property. While it produced a healthy crop, it took an exceedingly long time to develop.

The first full crop of this specially blended alfalfa was finally harvested and given to the farm animals. The very next day it started. Various animals began floating around. First, it was the sheep and goats. The farmers had to tie the goats to their fences, especially since once they commenced kicking, they kicked themselves right over to another field.

The following day the larger animals began to leave the ground including the cows and horses. Because of the problems this caused, it would be years before this crop blend would be repeated and grown on purpose. And then it was done to make the migration of the animals to the North Pole easier.

Following the great migration, it would be many more years before the crop would be grown again for Amerigo, and then regularly for the famous team of reindeer that you are about to read here.

This alfalfa grows in only one area in the world. Also unlike other types of alfalfa, it matures very slowly needing sometimes 6 or 7 months instead of 6 or 7 weeks like different varieties. So not as much can be produced, and of course, that is only as long as the weather cooperates. So barely enough is grown to put all but a small percentage of reindeer on it for any period.

This alfalfa is used only strictly for our flying reindeer and Amerigo, and mostly for a week or two at a time. Not only is this alfalfa rare, but it doesn't have all the minerals and vitamins that deer (and other animals) need to stay healthy if on it for too long.

So how does it work? It causes a weightless factor similar to the bones in birds. The bones become hollow, and the other organs lose much of their mass making the animal almost weightless.

The exciting thing is that even though the bones hollow out, they become stronger on the exterior and the muscles become tighter, lighter, but stronger as well.

That's the principle without getting too detailed. It should also be pointed out that the antlers on reindeer work exceptionally well with the jet streams to make them much faster than the speed of sound when needed.

Because the population of the world became so much more significant, and children who believed in Santa Claus became so many, we now use nine reindeer and a

giant sleigh to visit them all. I have all but retired
Amerigo, and now only use him for the eve of the Feast of
St. Nicholas.

So now, let's talk about the reindeer you all have heard
of from one time to another.

Dasher

Faster Than
a Missle

I have some extremely fast reindeer. And that's when they are on the ground. Give a few of those reindeer some of that unique blended alfalfa and a little training and look out! They can not only break the sound barrier, but they can go Mach 4 or 5 if they put it into overdrive.

We knew that Dasher would be one of my fastest from the moment he was born. The majority of newly born reindeer, whether calf or fawn, are always ungainly and can barely stand for their first couple days. But not Dasher, he was practically born standing and began walking within moments of his birth.

In fact, his mother had trouble cleaning him off because he was already in a hurry to explore his new world. Forrest Heademup, who is our Reindeer Wrangler and Range Boss, and my Dad couldn't believe what they were seeing. A newly born reindeer walking around as if he was several weeks old already. Dad named him Dasher right off.

As Dasher grew, he never "walked" anywhere. He always ran from place to place, as if he had to get to wherever he was going in the shortest amount of time. When my father decided to use reindeer to traverse the world, Dasher was one of his first picks to try a new concept.

He didn't disappoint. While he isn't the high stepper Dancer is, he is the fastest and one of the most active deer in the North Pole (although the twins are still stronger). His speed and agility are a joy to watch, and he is a blur unless he is standing still, which he never likes to do.

We hold races every year, more for fun than anything else. Dasher has placed first for every one of those years. All the reindeer look forward to trying to beat him, but none have been able to do so. There have been a couple close calls but they never make it all the way before Dasher overtakes them.

Dasher has been the point behind the red nosed reindeer on nearly all the Christmas Eve runs. He is still one of my favorites and always will be. He is also the deer I use on my private flights because I can always count on getting from point A to point B in the least possible time. Something that I enjoy almost as much as Dasher.

The Twins

Donner

&

Blitzen

What most people do not know outside the North Pole is that Donner and Blitzen are twin brothers. They were born minutes apart with Donner being the elder of the two by 18 minutes. More often than not, with most of the twins born to us, one is always more dominant. Such is not the case with these two. They are evenly matched and genuinely are identical in almost every way and are the strongest of my reindeer. I will say that Blitzen is more stubborn about a great many things, though he has a gentler side as well.

I named them after the thunderstorm that was taking place while they were being born. It was one of the loudest and most violent we had seen in the Pole. Their mother, Buttercup, began showing signs of labor in the afternoon, and the clouds started soon after. We moved Thor out of the stable, as it is never a good idea to keep the male around while the female is giving birth. It was a good thing we did because soon afterward came the first crack of lightning and as soon as the thunder came, Thor began rearing up and creating an awful fuss.

He indeed wasn't living up to his namesake, or maybe he was reacting because of it, but either way, it took Forrest Heademup and five other elves to keep him subdued. About that same time Buttercup laid down to have her babies. Since Forrest was wholly tied up with Thor, I was asked to help Buttercup.

Being a midwife to a reindeer is something I had done many times before and since. While we were inside the stable and safe from the storm, I was concerned that all the commotion and noise from this storm would complicate matters.

But Buttercup was a pro through it all, and she had both fawns without incident. They were beautiful and perfect in every reindeer way. Through the sheen of the birth, I could see they both carried their mother's reddish coat. Since I assisted in the delivery, I got to name them. I felt it fitting that since they came in a storm calling them, Thunder and Lightning was appropriate. But I used the German derivative of the names instead of the English version, especially since we already had a Lightning. So Thunder became Blitzen, and Lightning was Donner.

They both grew healthy and big. In fact, the twins became considerably larger and stronger than most of the other deer. And yet in spite of their size, they were remarkably nimble and fast. I watched them during the reindeer games many times and am still impressed with their speed, strength, agility and the fact that they always seem to move as one.

No matter what direction they go, they do it together. Each was matching the stride of the other. It was for this reason, (along with their size and strength) that I had decided to use the twins together and at the rear of the team for more "horsepower".

While they are strong enough to lead, I found that they give me that extra added power to get the sleigh moving as we take off. It's kind of like putting the engine of a jet in the rear for extra propulsion. Toward the end of my long flight, these two still have plenty of power to spare even as the other deer are showing signs of exhaustion.

I have used these two more times than any other reindeer in the team. And on the rare occasion I haven't, I have missed them. Talk about a matched set; even their antlers grow the same size and number of points (within a couple of tines) every year!

They both have sired many fawns and are often seen grazing and hanging around together most of the year, which is unusual for two big males like them.

I am pleased with these two, and I must say that while I have many favorite deer, Donner and Blitzen are at the top of the list.

So how do we tall them apart? It isn't easy, but fortunately, we use different colored harnesses on each. One wears dark red and the other a creamy white. Can you guess which might wear which?

Vixen

Our Most
Beautiful Reindeer

There is absolutely no doubt in anyone's mind at the North Pole as to which of our reindeer is the most beautiful. It is a hands-down conclusion that Vixen is our winner.

Vixen actually got her name shortly after being born. Even as a baby she had some very big and beautiful eyes with incredibly long eye lashes. She also has a pretty white spot on her head and a white tail, which always makes her stand out in the crowd. Her beautiful reddish-brown coat often glistens in the sun and shows off the white on her head and tail. But everyone comments about how pretty her eyes are. And it was Frederick Salsbury who made the statement "With eyes like those, she is going to be quite the vixen when she gets older."

Yes, sometimes that's just the way it happens. Someone will make a statement regarding a feature on the reindeer and the name sticks. In Frederick's case, it also became a prediction that held true. As soon as she started batting those pretty eyes, the bulls came running. It is really no surprise to any of us that she gets the most attention of any reindeer.

Vixen is not only beautiful, but also fast and nimble. Most times when she is on the sleigh, I hardly realize it because she moves so fluidly. No matter what deer I put next to her, she will always pull her own weight making both reindeer feel like one. Whenever she is participating in the reindeer games, she will outperform all but our best reindeer, regardless if they are boys or girls.

She is as fleet-footed as Dancer, as powerful as Comet, as durable Cupid, and as said earlier, the prettiest deer you may ever see. You can tell how proud she is to be one of the regulars for Christmas Eve. She always competes hard, proving that she deserves to be one of the nine reindeer I use consistently.

Our biggest problem is all the boys want to try and impress Vixen and will go out of their way to look and act stronger. Many times this adversely affects the team as a whole and throws everything off kilter. This problem is why I always put another girl with Vixen to keep everything running smoothly. As most people know, I will pair her with Prancer. The two girls make an excellent pair and have incredible stamina and poise.

It is amazing how just two pairs of legs can throw the entire team and sleigh out of balance. When you are covering thousands upon thousands of miles over two days, anything that keeps us from performing at peak optimum might prevent us from finishing our rounds!

People are always surprised to learn that Prancer is a female. She is also a lovely reindeer and when paired with Vixen, watching them run is poetry in motion. Another reindeer I may use with Vixen is Snowfire. As her name suggests, Snowfire is a brilliant all-white reindeer, and the two make a stunning pair on the team. I use her when either Prancer or Vixen aren't up to making the long trip.

When you see my sleigh look for a reindeer with big beautiful eyes and a white spot. If you see her, consider yourself lucky indeed, because it is a rare sight at Christmas to see Vixen.

Comet
The Long
Tailed Reindeer

We name some reindeer for their strength, some for their speed, and many get their names because of a unique feature they have. Comet's name came from two of the above reasons. He, along with Fireball, Jet, Rocket, and Cougar, is one of my fastest reindeer (although, not quite as fast as Dasher). The first time I used him on the Christmas Eve run I had to slow him down continually, so he didn't outrun his hitch-mate. It took a couple of times, but I found a couple of especially good deer to keep pace with him.

Comet, along with the twins, also have the best stamina of all the reindeer. He could run for days if I needed him to, and as the team gets tired heading into the early morning, that's when I rely on Comet to give that extra energy required to finish the delivery.

I can never put him on the front though, as he would wear out the rest of the team before we were halfway through. So I keep him generally in the number five or six position depending on his hitch-mate, always around the middle of the team for that extra punch. But as to how he got his name?

When he was born, he had one unusual feature that you couldn't help but immediately notice. He had the most extended tail ever seen on a reindeer! When he was born, his tail was almost as long as his legs. The coloration was like an average reindeer's tail, brown on top and light gray underneath, but it was as long as an adult fox's tail. You were even able to see it from the front because it hung so far down. Well, Forrest Heademup commented that it was as long as a comet's tail. And from that moment on, that became his name.

Now as is often the case in nature, sometimes you are born with an unusually large feature like a long nose or large ears, but you eventually grow into them over time. And such was the case with Comet. All his young days he carried this enormous flag on his rump, but after the first year it was more proportional, and he grew into an extremely large and handsome reindeer. However, he still has one of the most magnificent tails you will ever see on a reindeer.

What surprised everyone is what came later. Reindeer develop patterns and coloration's once they become adults. In addition to his long brown and white tail, Comet's coat developed an unusual design along his side. As he runs in the night sky with his tail straight out behind him, he absolutely looks like a comet! With white on his broad shoulder that extends his entire length and narrows toward his white rear, he is Comet the comet! So when you see my sleigh, just look for the reindeer that resembles his name the most, and you will spot him right off.

He has certainly proved his value and worth over the many generations, and he still holds the record for the longest tail born to a reindeer in the North Pole.

Cupid

The

Escape

Artist

There is one of my more famous reindeer who likes to challenge us with his antics. When he was first born, we gave him a different name, but by the time he reached adulthood, we decided to officially change it to the nickname the elves repeatedly called him.

Cupid continuously roams to other stalls in the stable, and other parts of the Pole. Specifically, to wherever his friends and fellow reindeer are. It is nearly impossible to keep him from bouncing and flying all over the North Pole.

Long ago when he was first born to Paprika and Glacier, I was worried that like his father he would be a sturdy but very slow reindeer (Glacier, as in 'moves like a...'). I suspected that Cupid might be one of those reindeer that would end up pulling a mail sled or moving shipments from the train station to other parts of the Pole. Something suited to a slower pace.

When he grew to be an adult, I was amazed to find how fast he moved. You would see him cover great distances in no time. He would bound from place to place like any of my best coursers. In addition to being fast, Cupid is also a beautiful reindeer with an attractive white patch on his head, a white nose, and a thick brown coat. So I decided to give him a tryout on flying to see if he would work out for Christmas Eve.

There was no disappointment there; Cupid took to flying like a duck takes to water. Soon he was leaping into the air and going from one end of the Pole to the other like a shot. That's when all the trouble started.

You see, Cupid loved to visit his friends and hitch-mates. He would leap from one end of the Pole to the other to meet another reindeer. He was the incurable escape artist, and we could never keep him penned. Most of the reindeer didn't have a problem when Cupid came calling. But it disrupted all the work getting done because the other reindeer were supposed to be working and not socializing.

This also made some of the deer jealous that Cupid could always escape, and they weren't able to do it. So some took issue with Cupid. And for a time it seemed that the elves had to spend too much effort preventing Cupid from traveling all around the village. He would even find ways out of his stall at night and "go wandering." For a while, we had to post someone at his paddock all night long until we could figure out how he was getting free. It was the only way to keep Cupid from going out on his nightly forays.

The first time I used him for the Christmas Eve trip, he did very well. I put him with a more experienced reindeer (Blaze), and he pulled his weight with the others without issue. The next year I teamed him with Cinnamon, one of my prettiest females, and found out what a disaster that was!

That had to be the hardest Christmas Eve trip of my life – and that is saying something when you think how many times I have done this. I usually have a couple of missteps every Christmas Eve, but this was ridiculous! Cupid never left Cinnamon alone. He was continually trying to nuzzle and bother her, which she didn't appreciate one bit. And in their full harnesses, they kept getting tangled, causing me to stop and straighten everything out too often to count.

It was years before I used Cupid again. Then came the year where it seemed that I had lost every courser to a variety of problems. From being sick to losing antlers early, to having new fawns or calves, I had scraped the bottom of the barrel for reindeer for my Christmas Eve team. I finally decided to use Cupid again, but this time I paired him with Comet, a somewhat new reindeer, that I had used a few times with satisfying results.

What a perfect pair! They worked together effortlessly, and they became two of the best reindeer I ever had on the team. I have used them together year after year since, and always with the same happy results. Being close friends, this is one of the reindeer Cupid likes to visit most.

Now that Cupid is older, he has slowed in "making his rounds." He still gets free, and we can't always figure out how he escapes.

But chances are still strong that if we are looking for Cupid, we never have to search any further than the closest reindeer friend of his.

Prancer

Santa's Proudest Reindeer

Sometimes you get lucky and name something correctly. That happened with our Prancer. Most reindeer when they are first born are very unsteady on their feet for a little while. Even when produced in the wild, the parents have to help the young reindeer get and keep moving. Not Prancer. From the moment she was born she stood on all fours was rock steady.

No actually more than that. Prancer seemed to be high-stepping and loved to bounce about or, prance. She had a grace and sureness about her every step. When she became older, she could dance rings around most of the other reindeer. She had a beautiful coat of dark brown that she got from her father, Pocatello. Pocatello also sired another of Santa's more famous reindeer, Rudolph. Though Rudolph had a different mother, so Prancer is his half-sister.

Prancer was built for flying and loves it as much any of her hitch-mates. She is one of the proudest reindeer in the team. She gets along exceedingly well with all the other reindeer, and I always put her immediately behind another with dancing feet like Prancer. They even rhyme together – Dancer and Prancer. Dancer is another reindeer with lighter than air hooves.

The two will prance and dance about because they are always ready to go, and they give the elves a hard time until firmly hitched to the sleigh. I lose more bells from these two because they are continuously in motion. They always seem to rub against the other reindeer and loosen the jingle bells if not secured tightly. Most people already know I usually have her hitched to Vixen because they work so well together.

Prancer is one of my more frequently used reindeer, but I will also switch her hitch-mate, sometimes replacing either Vixen or her with Ginger or Cinnamon, two of my other females when needed. Such as when either Prancer or Vixen are having a baby, which is sometimes the case for one or the other, if not both at the same time.

Prancer always adapts well, and is very proud to be part of the team. On the trips I do not use her, she pouts for a day or so and then begin to prance about the Pole as usual. While she is getting older now, Prancer still can move better than most of my younger deer. She has had many sons and daughters of her own over the many years, and I have even used a few of them on the sleigh team as well. They too have their mother's pride.

But no matter how many times I make this trip, when Prancer is not in the third position, it doesn't feel quite right. So, I plan to continue with my proudest reindeer for many more years to come.

Dancer

Santa's Dancing Reindeer

Every single year, with rare exception, hitched in front and to the right of my team is my highest stepping reindeer. When I first put Dancer on the sleigh team, he would accidentally kick the deer in front of him because he took such long, high steps. While he has strong legs and is fast, he also has exceptional strides and would get tangled up in the harnesses. The tangling always happened if I place him in any other position than the number one or two slots directly behind my red nosed reindeer (more on that later).

One year he got so wrapped up it took me over an hour to get everything back to the way it should be, only to get tangled again in the next country. Once we moved him to the front position, he worked out beautifully.

Dancer has an excellent countenance and is a gorgeous looking reindeer. He and Prancer are my two "prancing" reindeer. They both love to 'kick up their hooves' but Dancer can high-step like no other. From the time he was born we saw he had a remarkable stride for a reindeer. He was a little shaky for a day or two, but then after that, every day he acted as if he was marching in a parade.

He 'dances' in front of all the females and they obviously enjoy his moves, as he has sired many reindeer over the years. His overall color is a very dark chestnut, and he has tiny 'socks' around his hooves. He has very few distinguishing features which are unusual in itself. From the tip of his antlers to his socks he is a very dark brown. He has the smallest patch of white on the very tip of his nose. He also has a splash of white on his chest and rump, but from the side, he almost looks solid brown. Even more unusual is that his coat never varies regardless of the season. It always is that rich cocoa color all year.

You will know Dancer right off, as he almost always is in the front on my right. You can tell it is him because he is always moving. Even when stopped on top of the roof, he is still "Dancing." But because of his dark coat, he can be hard to see from a distance on the roof.

Speaking of roofs, sometimes it is hard to tell where the roof ends and Dancer begins. Even with another reindeer in front of him, I have to be particularly careful on especially dark nights. It can be difficult to see. Of course, all of my reindeer know where the roof-line ends and will always make sure not to overshoot the distance.

When I have Dancer in the front, I never have to worry much about how smoothly we will get the job done. So please leave a carrot for one of my best reindeer, or better still he loves bananas more!

The Other
Red Nosed
Reindeer

It's a good thing reindeer don't suffer from ego problems the way humans do. Imagine continuously being called by another name? How would you feel never being given credit for the work you do? Not to mention having people always singing a song about someone else and never you. Torch, one of my other Red-Nosed Reindeer, gets it all the time. Poor guy, he has now lead the team during many a Christmas Eve. In fact almost as often that "Famous One" as we like to call him up here (in order not to keep using his name in front of the other reindeer).

I like to switch off every other year or so. You see some years, "Famous One's" antlers get so vast that the wind plays havoc with them, and that means it plays havoc with the whole team. So thankfully we have four RN's (red nosed) to switch off when needed or preferred.

Only two of the others had been born to the Pole, our fourth one was seen running with a Chukotka herd around Finland, and we were able to bring him here after quite a chase. His name is Strobe. The last of the four is Flash. What? Never heard of them? Well, that's little surprise, it wasn't until the 1830's that people even learned I used reindeer.

That was when Dr. Clement Clarke Moore penned a poem "A Visit With St. Nicholas". It was almost one hundred years later (1937) when Rudolph's song came into being. We continue to hope that with four male RN's, they will produce more, but so far, while we have some beautiful reindeer none have had the RN gene.

But I digress. This subject is about Torch, one of our other beautiful RN's. He was born to Blizzard and Snowflake around the latter half of the last century. He was a sturdy and pretty reindeer from the onset. We had a major festival and celebrated his March 7th birth for weeks. He grew fast and was soon entered into the reindeer games to begin his training. He built stamina quickly, and soon was giving the seasoned veterans a run for their money. We used him as the lead reindeer for the first time in 1989.

It takes years of training to make the team, and while I often need to switch out other reindeer, I only use extensively trained stock. Being Santa Claus, I cannot afford a mistake on my tight delivery schedule, and we will not disappoint any children by not making their delivery on Christmas Eve. As our Chief Reindeer Wrangler Forrest Heademup predicted, Torch performed magnificently, and I was relieved to know I officially had another backup.

So what causes a red nose in the first place? It is a unique pigment that is hereditary. Just as some people are born with blond hair and blue eyes and others with red hair and green eyes, some reindeer are born as albinos (pure white), and others have red noses. Nearly every reindeer is born with fur on their nose which is black underneath, but a red nose is a light leathery nose, and the pigments underneath cause light similar to a firefly, or more like a black dragonfish that produces a red glow through bioluminescence.

Fireflies, anglerfish, and other creatures produce the chemicals luciferin (a pigment) and luciferase (an enzyme). The luciferin reacts with oxygen to create light. Clearly, with a reindeer's nose, it is the first place to get oxygen, and that is where the pigment is brightest. Sorry, I didn't mean to get so technical, but many don't realize what a common occurrence in nature this is. It is extremely rare in reindeer, and so far as I know, this is the most significant animal that carries the luciferin gene.

Because of the size of the nose and pigments involved, it can be extremely bright! Just like with other animals, the deer control it. So when I call out for 'full power', they can illuminate my way during the darkest night. But other times it can be barely noticeable, as when the reindeer are asleep or wish to go unnoticed. When in their "dark" mode they are hard to find in the wild. Most reindeer will not call attention to themselves. But that was how we found Strobe. He was running in front of the herd, and they were all following him because he could see through the blowing snow using his extremely brilliant nose.

As appearances go, Torch looks similar to Rudolph in

size, and of course with his nose, especially from a distance. But he has very distinct features of his own. For one, his stockings are much longer than Rudolph's going almost seven inches up his leg from his hooves. Also, Torch is a darker gray versus Rudolph's lighter reddish-tan. Torch's antlers can get up to 30 points or more. Rudolph can still grow a bigger rack, sometimes reaching the 40 point range. But that's when I need Torch, Strobe or Flash the most. That number of points works like too many sails on a ship; they will begin working against each other fighting the jet stream instead of flowing with it.

So the next time you look into the sky for my magical team and me, please remember, it might be Torch you are looking for and not that "Famous One". Maybe someday the other three will have songs about them, But never fear, they will do fine without one.

Closing Message From Santa Claus

Well, now you know about my more famous reindeer. Before I leave you, I must tell you that there is one person who knows more about reindeer than even I do. His name is Forrest Heademup, and as I said earlier, he is my Chief Reindeer Wrangler. Although his title scarcely explains Forrest and his duties.

Not only is he in charge of the reindeer, but he knows and takes care of all the animals in the North Pole and beyond. To learn about Forrest, you can read *Glaciers Melt & Mountains Smoke*, as he is a principal character in that book. You may be surprised to learn about the variety of animals that reside with us, and Forrest helps manage them all.

Speaking of books, if you have enjoyed this, the author has written many more. You have the opportunity to delve into an entirely new world involving Santa and Mrs. Claus, the elves, animals, and goings on of the North Pole and then the move to an entirely new location.

The entire family will enjoy traveling with Santa and Mrs. Claus in the Santa Claus Trilogy. The books of this trilogy are *Believe Again, The North Pole Chronicles, Faith, Hope & Reindeer, and Glaciers Melt & Mountains Smoke.*

And for toddlers through early grades, North Pole Press offers a distinctive collection about the special elves that help Santa Claus entitled Santa's Elf Series©. A long time ago Santa Claus met his elves. They offered to help make his dream a reality of bringing gifts and toys to children throughout the world. Now the stories of these remarkable helpers are finally told through this series that helps young readers learn to read through rhyme and beautiful illustrations. At the end of each book is a very special message from Santa on how to stay on his "nice" list.

The Santa's Elf Series series begins with Santa's World and will have twelve books when completed.

Other books already available in the series include:
Jamie Hardrock, Santa's Chief Mining Elf
Shelley Wrapitup, Master Design Elf
Keeney Eagleye, Naughty/Nice List Manager
Sarah Buttons, Master Doll Maker
Ford MacHarley, Master Wheelsmith

And more elves will follow. Each book is available through the North Pole Press at www.thenorthpolepress.com. And check out the other books by this diverse author, he has written several more.